Franklin
WANTS A PET

Franklin and the Franklin characters are trademarks of Kids Can Press Ltd.

Kids Can Press is a Nelvana company.

ISBN 0-439-35499-4

Text copyright © 1995 by Contextx Inc.
Illustrations copyright © 1995 by Brenda Clark Illustrator Inc.

Illustrations prepared with the assistance of Lynn Adams.

12 11 10 9 8 7 6 5 4 3 2 1   1 2 3 4 5 6/0
Printed in Singapore   46

First Scholastic printing, January 1995
First Scholastic miniature edition printing, October 2001

Franklin
WANTS A PET

Paulette Bourgeois • Brenda Clark

SCHOLASTIC INC.

New York   Toronto   London   Auckland   Sydney
Mexico City   New Delhi   Hong Kong   Buenos Aires

FRANKLIN could count by twos and tie his shoes. He could sleep alone in his small, dark shell. He even had a best friend named Bear. But Franklin wanted something else. He wanted a pet.

Franklin had wanted a pet since he was small. But whenever he asked, "May I have a pet, please?" his parents said, "Maybe someday."

Franklin waited for a long time. He often pretended to have a pet. He took Sam, his stuffed dog, for walks. He taught Sam tricks. He even helped Sam bury some bones. But Sam wasn't a real pet.

One day, Franklin asked his parents again,
"May I have a pet, please?"

Franklin's parents looked at each other.

"We'll think about it," they answered.

At first, Franklin was happy because they did
not say, *No.* Then, Franklin became worried. His
parents could think about things for days and days.

That day, Franklin visited Bear and told him all about the pet he wanted.

"If I had a pet, it would be a bird," said Bear.

"Why?" asked Franklin.

"Because birds sing beautiful songs," said Bear.

"Birds are nice," said Franklin. "But their loud singing may wake me too early."

Franklin waited until morning before asking his parents if they had finished thinking yet.

"Not quite," said Franklin's mother. "We need to know that you could care for a pet."

Franklin nodded his head up and down.

"Could you feed your pet?" asked Franklin's father.

Franklin nodded again. He almost said please one hundred times in a row but he stopped himself.

Franklin visited Beaver and told her all about the pet he wanted.

"If I had a pet it would be a cat," said Beaver.

"Why?" asked Franklin.

"Because cats make purring sounds," she answered.

"Cats are nice," said Franklin. "But you never know where they are."

Later that day, Franklin asked his parents, "Are you finished thinking?"

"Not yet," they answered.

"Please hurry," said Franklin.

His father sighed. "Franklin, this is a big decision. A pet costs money to buy and to keep."

Franklin offered all the money in his piggy bank and hoped it was enough.

After counting his pennies, Franklin visited with Goose and told her all about the pet he wanted.

"If I had a pet, it would be a bunny," said Goose.

"Why?" asked Franklin.

"Because bunnies have wiggly whiskers."

"Bunnies are nice," said Franklin. "But I think whiskers might make me sneeze."

After three whole days, Franklin was tired of
waiting for his parents to finish thinking. He had
a plan!

He brought Sam to the breakfast table. "I have
been taking care of Sam for a long, long time,"
he said. "I will take good care of a real pet, too.
I will feed it. I will clean its house. We can take it
to the vet if it gets sick."

Franklin's parents smiled. "It sounds as if you've
been doing a lot of thinking, too," they said.

"So may I have a pet, please?" he begged.

They whispered to each other. Then they nodded their heads up and down.

"Oh, thank you," said Franklin. He wanted to go to the pet store right away.

"We'll help you choose a puppy tomorrow," said his father.

"No thank you," said Franklin. "I do not want
a dog."

His parents were surprised.

"Dogs are nice," said Franklin. "But I want a
quiet pet."

Franklin's mother asked if he wanted a kitten.

"No thank you," said Franklin. "Kittens are nice
but I want a pet that stays close by."

"Is it a hamster that you want?" said Franklin's father.

Franklin shook his head. "No thank you."

"A rabbit?" asked Franklin's mother.

"No thank you," said Franklin.

"What kind of pet do you want?" asked his parents.

Franklin smiled and said, "I'll show you tomorrow."

At the pet store, Franklin pointed to a fish.

"I want a goldfish," he said.

"A goldfish!" they said. "Why? A fish cannot do tricks or play with you."

So Franklin explained. He liked to watch fish swim slowly around and around. He liked their beautiful colors. And he liked the way they made him feel inside. Quiet and calm.

"Besides," he said, "I love goldfish."

"That's the best reason of all," said Franklin's parents.

Franklin named his fish Goldie. He took very good care of her, just as he'd promised.

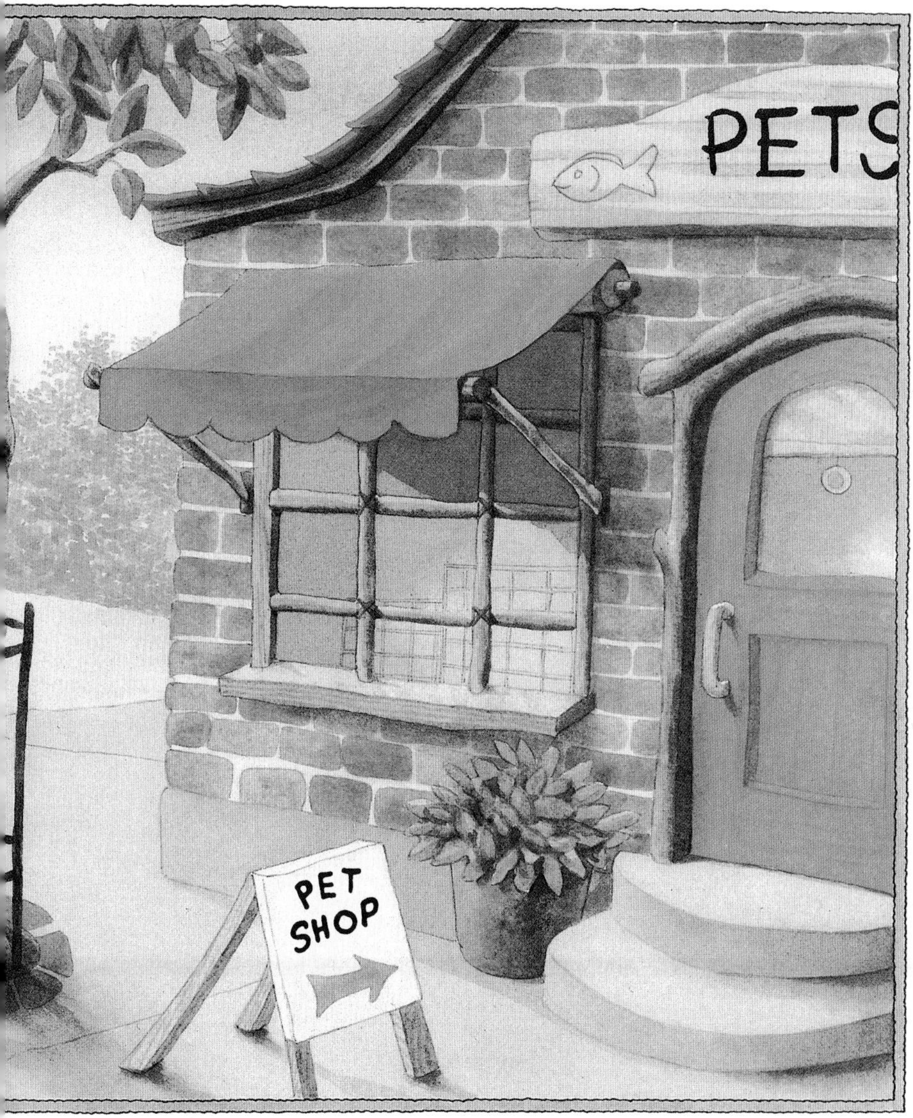
PETS
PET
SHOP

Every morning, Franklin watched Goldie swim around and around. And every night before he went to bed, Franklin blew a great big fish kiss and whispered, "I love you, Goldie."